MATH ADVENTURES

CARA COUNTS AT THE COUNTY FAIR

AN ADDITION ADVENTURE

by Megan Atwood
illustrated by Amy Zhing

GRASSHOPPER

Tools for Parents & Teachers

Grasshopper Books enhance imagination and introduce the earliest readers to fiction with fun storylines and illustrations. The easy-to-read text supports early reading experiences with repetitive sentence patterns and sight words.

Before Reading

- Look at the cover illustration. What do readers see? What do they think the book will be about?
- Look at the picture glossary together. Sound out the words. Ask readers to identify the first letter of each vocabulary word.

Read the Book

- "Walk" through the book, reading to or along with the reader. Point to the illustrations as you read.

After Reading

- Review the picture glossary again. Ask readers to locate the words in the text.
- Ask the reader: Cara counts animals at the fair. She counts tickets, too. What have you counted today?

Grasshopper Books are published by Jump!
5357 Penn Avenue South
Minneapolis, MN 55419
www.jumplibrary.com

Library of Congress Cataloging-in-Publication Data

Names: Atwood, Megan, author. | Zhing, Amy, illustrator.
Title: Cara counts at the county fair: an addition adventure / by Megan Atwood; illustrated by Amy Zhing.
Description: Minneapolis, MN: Jump!, Inc., [2022]
Series: Math adventures
Audience: Ages 4-7.
Identifiers: LCCN 2021038869 (print)
LCCN 2021038870 (ebook)
ISBN 9781636906294 (hardcover)
ISBN 9781636906300 (paperback)
ISBN 9781636906317 (ebook)
Subjects: LCSH: Readers (Primary)
Counting–Juvenile fiction.
LCGFT: Readers (Publications)
Classification: LCC PE1119.2 .A893 2022 (print)
LCC PE1119.2 (ebook) | DDC 428.6/2–dc23
LC record available at https://lccn.loc.gov/2021038869
LC ebook record available at https://lccn.loc.gov/2021038870

Editor: Eliza Leahy
Direction and Layout: Anna Peterson
Illustrator: Amy Zhing

Printed in the United States of America at Corporate Graphics in North Mankato, Minnesota.

Table of Contents

Counting Tickets

"I love the fair!" Cara says.

Cara counts the animals.

"One cow. Two chickens.
One goat," she says.
"That makes four animals!"

Cara wants to win a prize.

She buys two tickets for the balloon game.

She buys two tickets for the ring toss.

She buys two tickets for a ride.

TS
2 + 2 + 2 = 6

Cara plays the balloon game.

She pops one balloon.

Then she pops three more!

"I get four prize tickets!" she says.

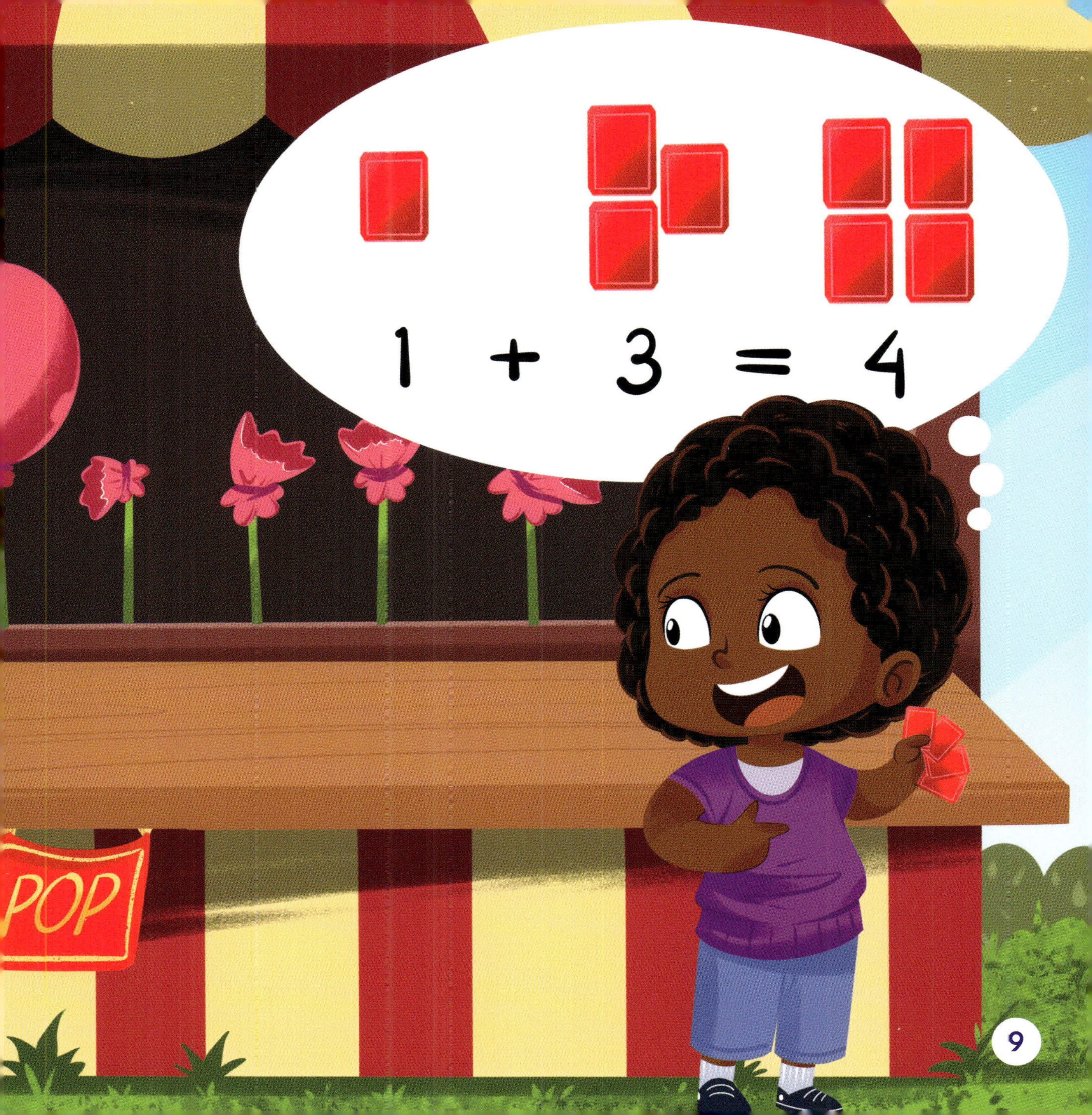
1 + 3 = 4
POP

Cara plays ring toss.

She throws one ring.
It lands on the cow.

Two rings land
on the chicken.

Three rings land
on the goat.

"I get six more tickets!"
Cara says.

1 + 2 + 3 = 6

Cara counts her prize tickets.

She has ten total!

“I can buy a teddy bear!”
Cara says.

Cara goes on a ride.

She counts the animals.

"One cow. Two chickens. One goat. That makes four animals," she says.

She looks at her teddy bear. "And you make five!"

1 + 2 + 1 + 1 = 5

Let's Review!

Cara saw several animals at the fair. How many times does the goat appear in the book?

A. seven times **B.** three times **C.** ten times **D.** five times

Picture Glossary

fair
An outdoor show of farm products and animals, often with food, games, and rides.

prize
A reward that is given to the winner of something.

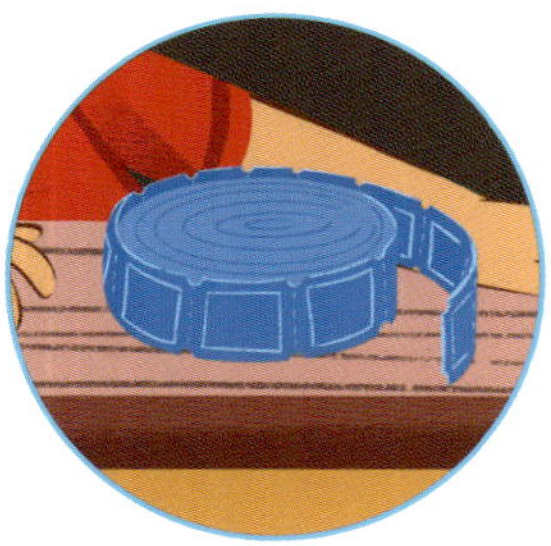

tickets
Pieces of paper that people can use to buy things.

total
Making up the whole amount.

Let's Review! Answer Key: **D.** five times